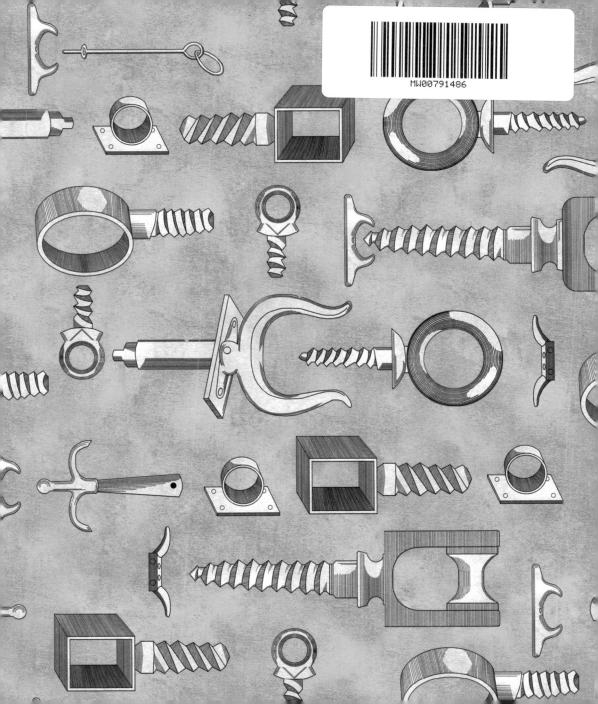

MW00791486

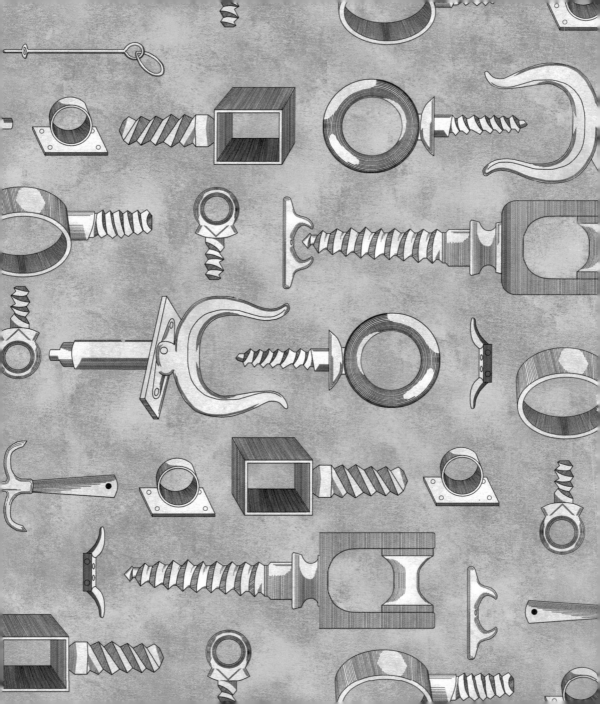

CHESTER 5000 XYV

for Stacey

♥ JESS FINK

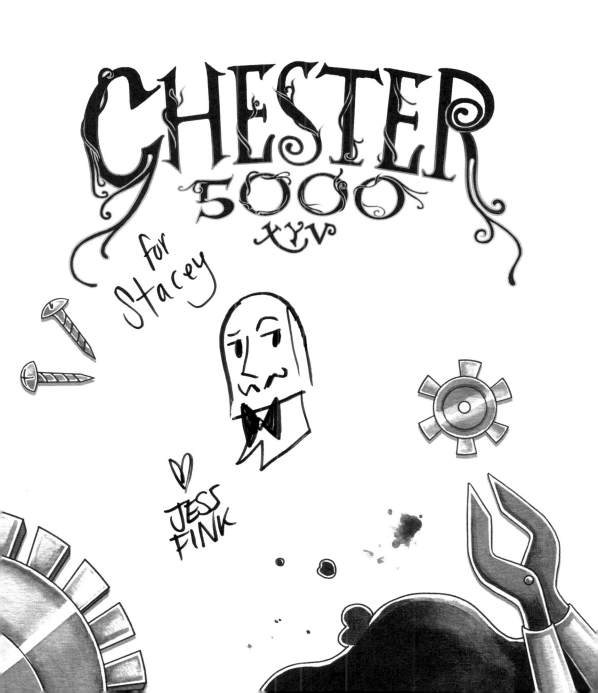

For eric and for Love

CHESTER
5,000
XYV!

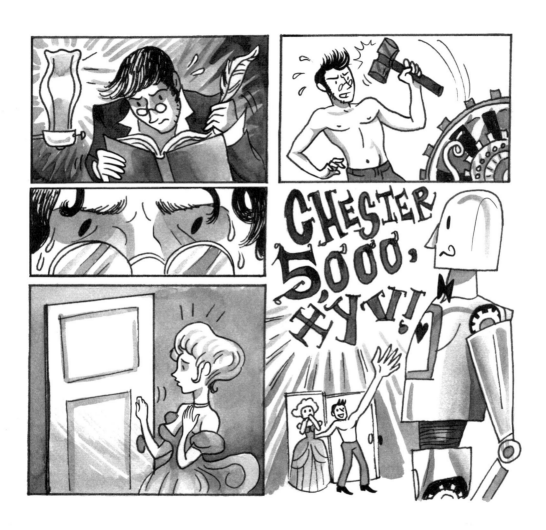

CLICK

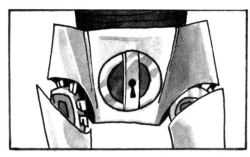

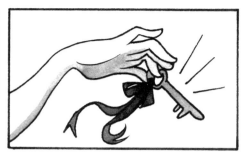

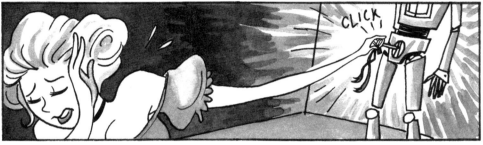

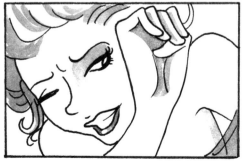

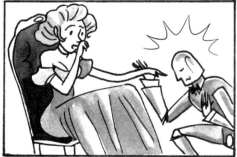

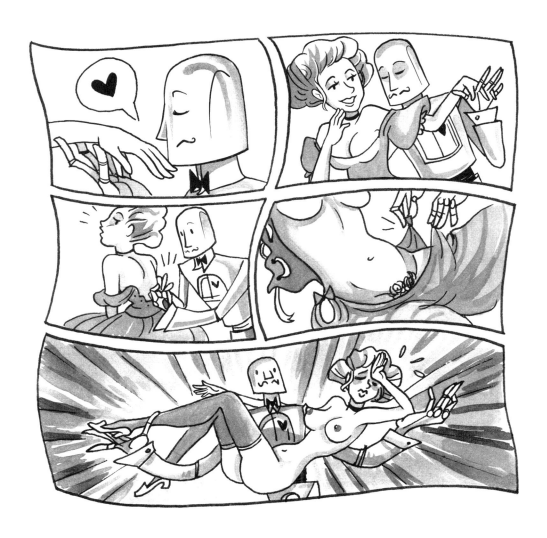

CLICK!
VERT!

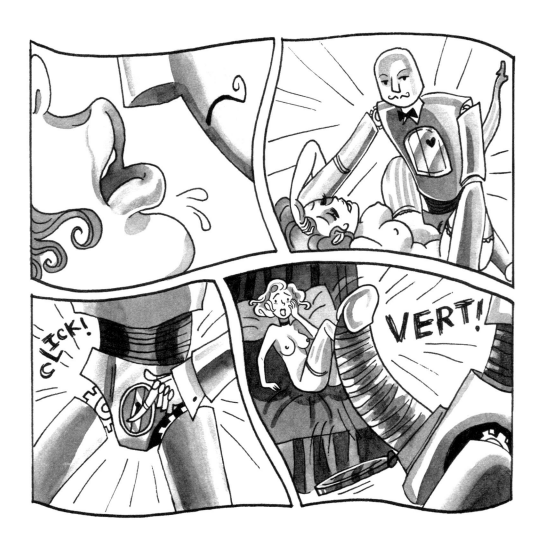

SLAM

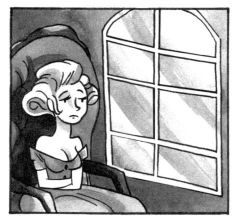

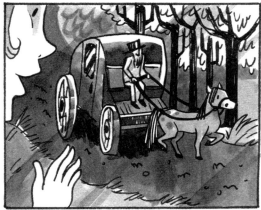

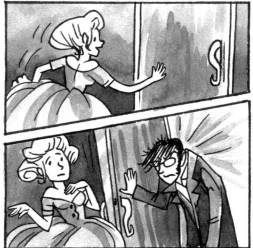

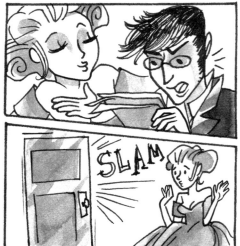

x=y?

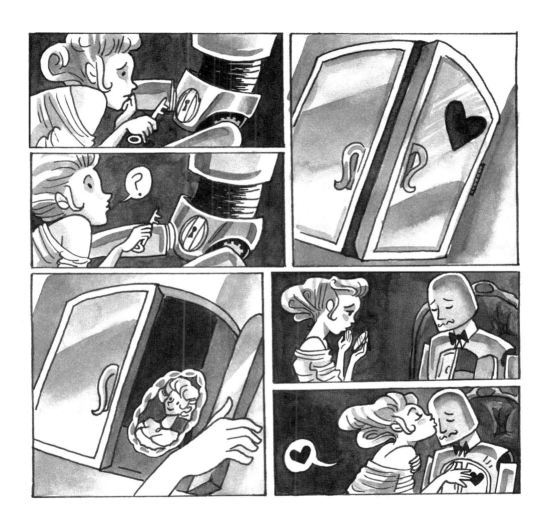

VERT

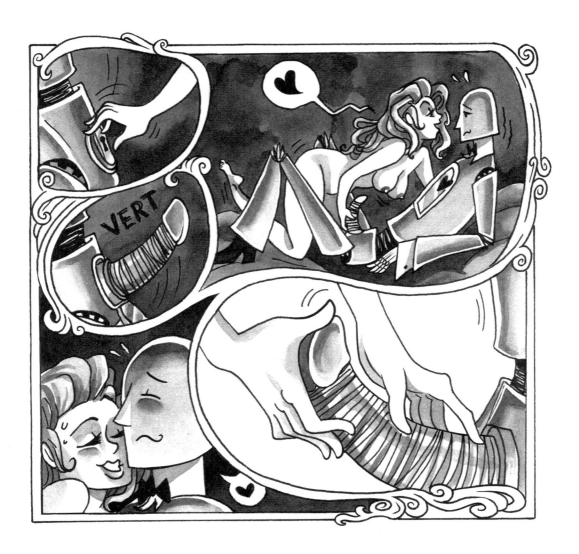

WOOOOP

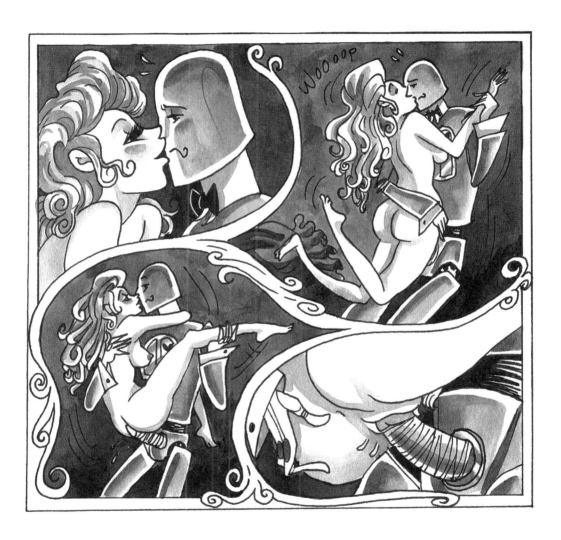

VERT
VERT
VERT
VERT
VERT

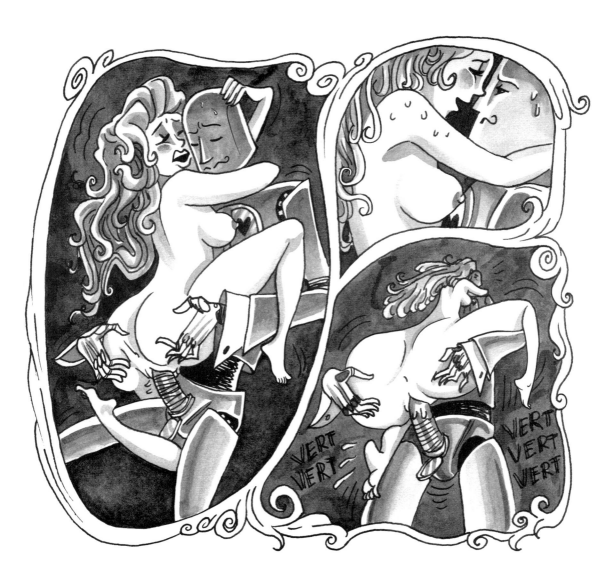

VERT!

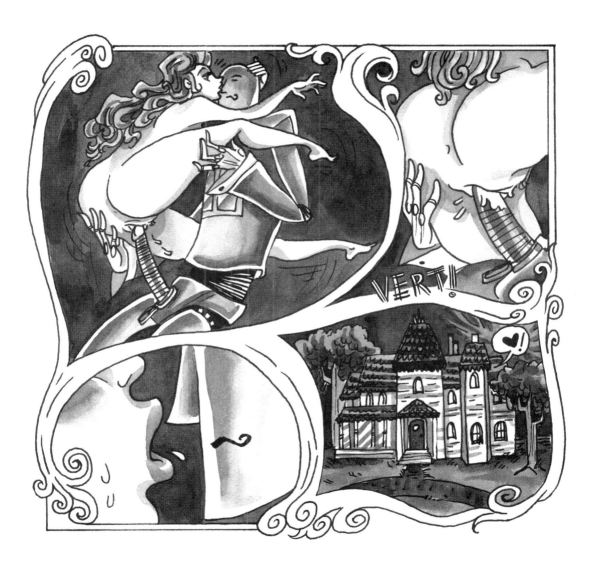

VERT!

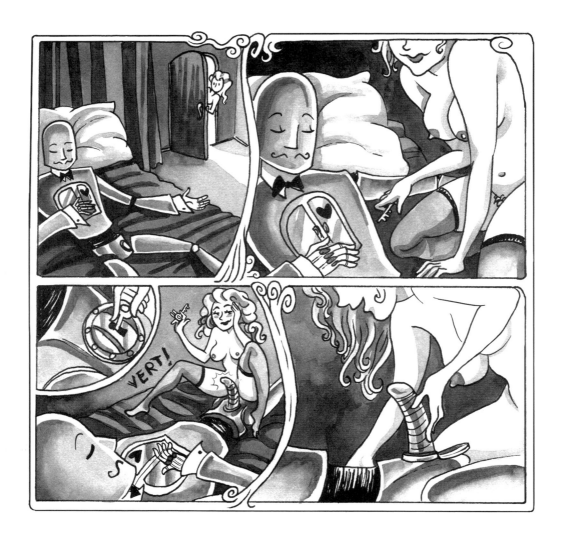

CRASH
BANG!!
POP
PECK
HA
HA!

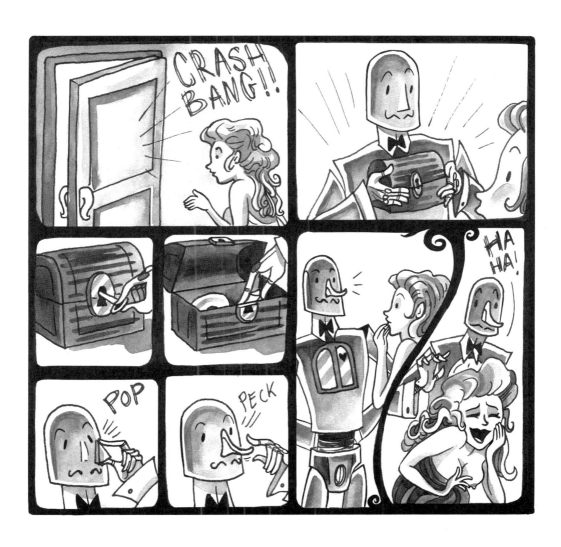

fig. 1
4 inches
2 inches
The Cunnilingua Nasum
Soft, Spongy Surface

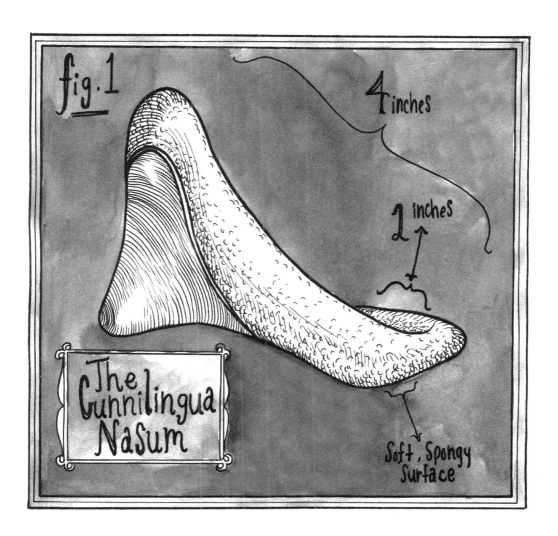

Lap Lap
Lap Lap

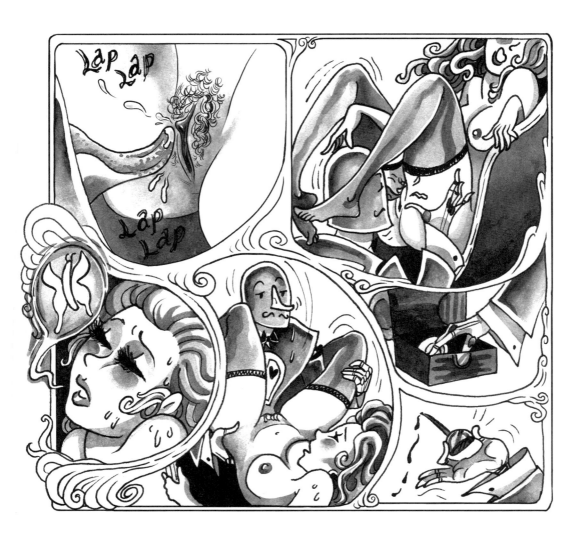

DoK
DoK

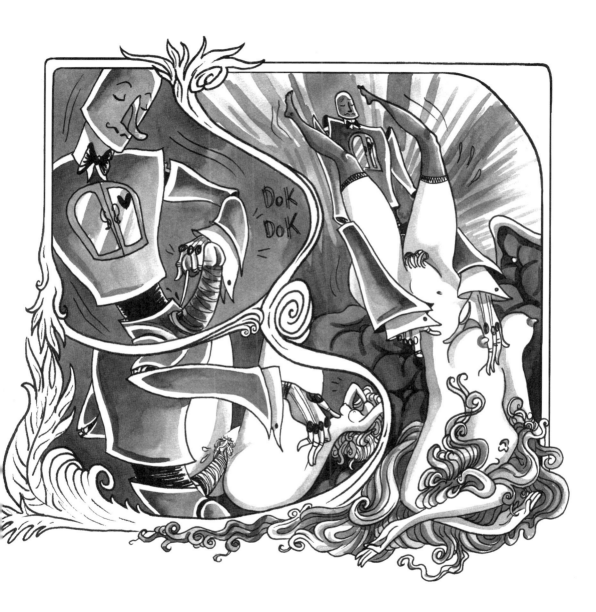

SPWOOOO
!!!

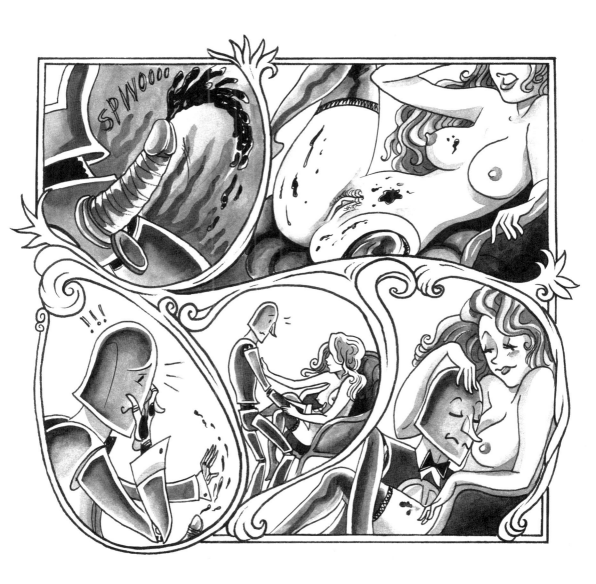

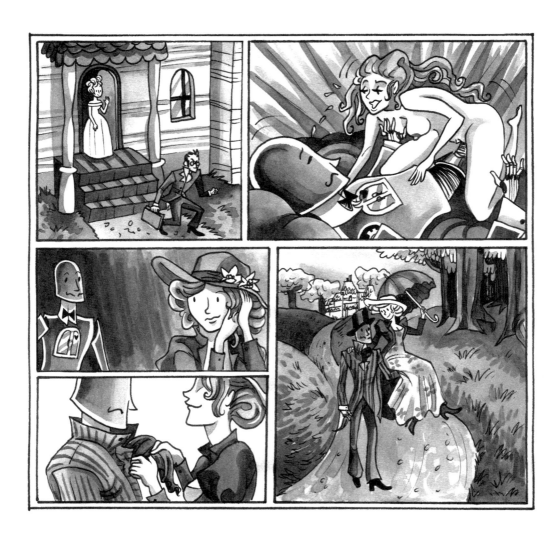

!!!
VRRRRRT

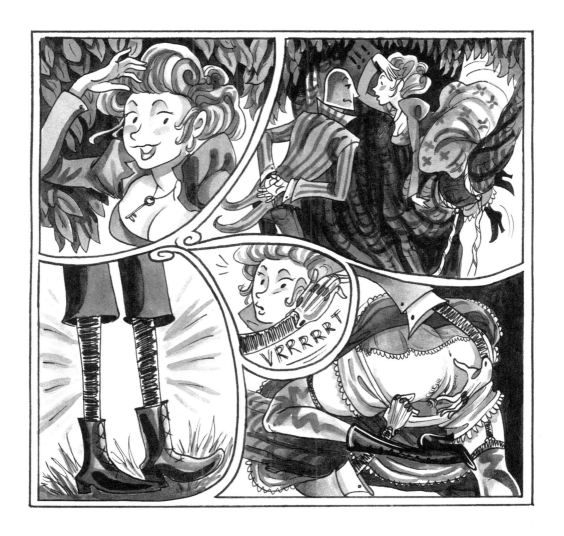

Extendo Limbus
Pearl cuff-link bolts
Interlocking curcular steel
5½ Feet
fig. 2

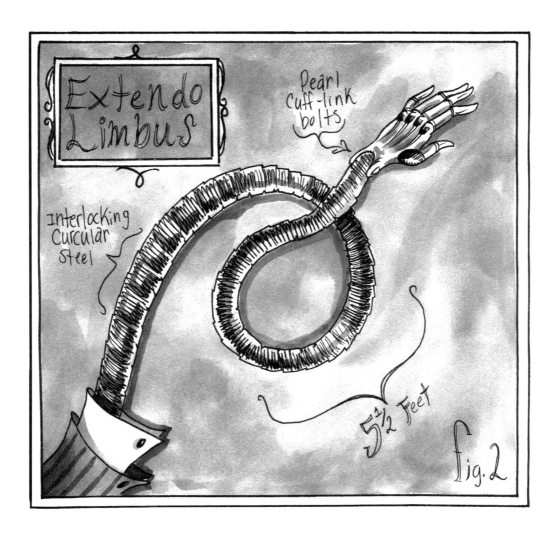

44

VERT !!

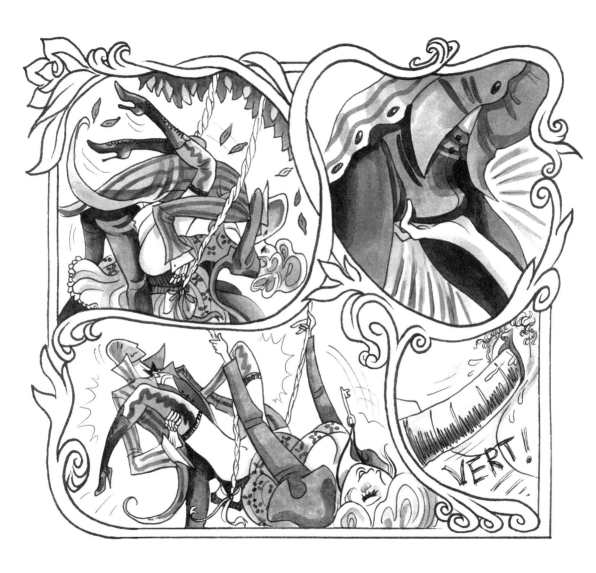

CLOP
CLOP

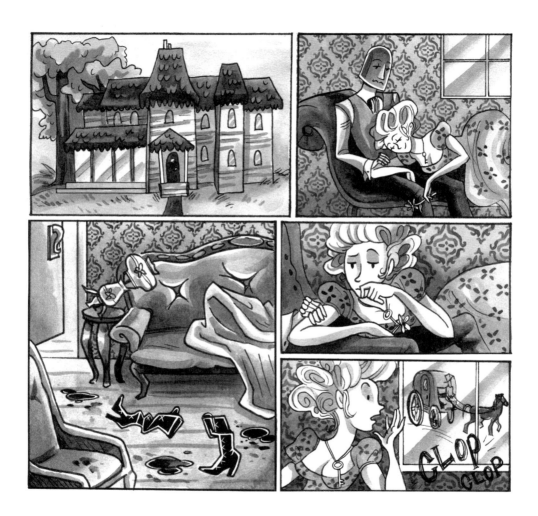

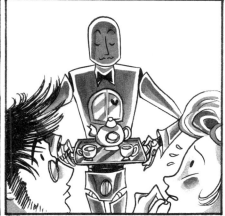

WOOOOOP

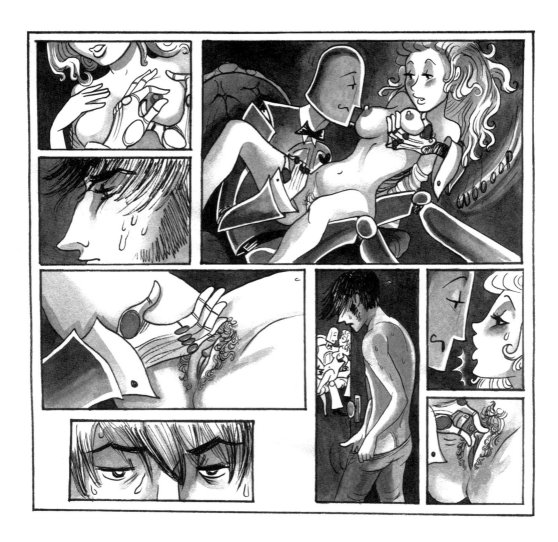

fig. 3
Vibrating tips
Stainless Steal
Vibratus fingum
Heat Sensitive

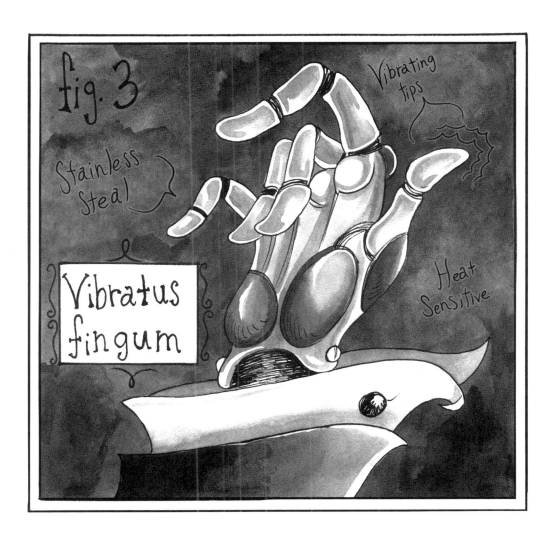

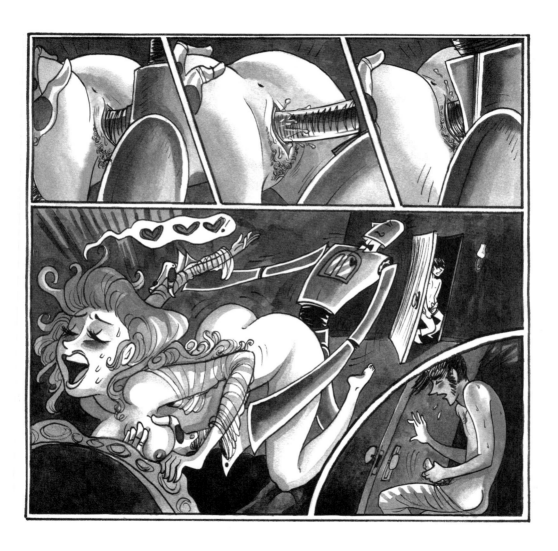

BANG
Knock
Knock
Knock
Knock
Knock
WHAM

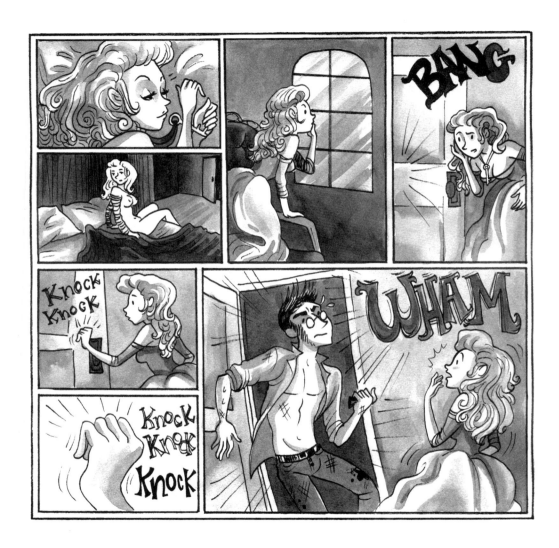

!!!
♥!?
SNAP

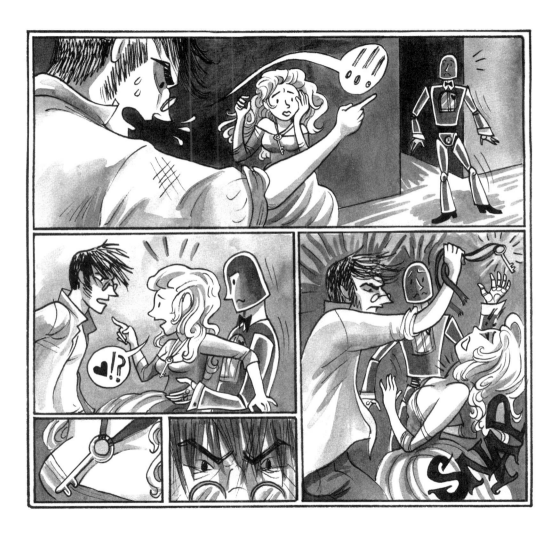

CLICK!
SHOOOOOOOM

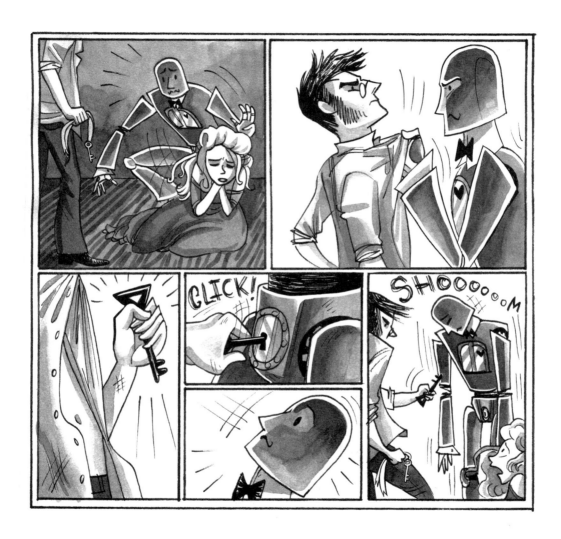

!?
WIKKA WIKKA
!
CLICK

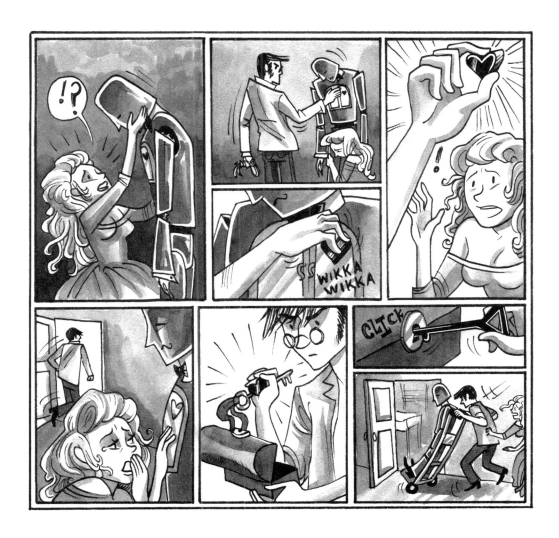

CLICK
?!
SLAM
?
!

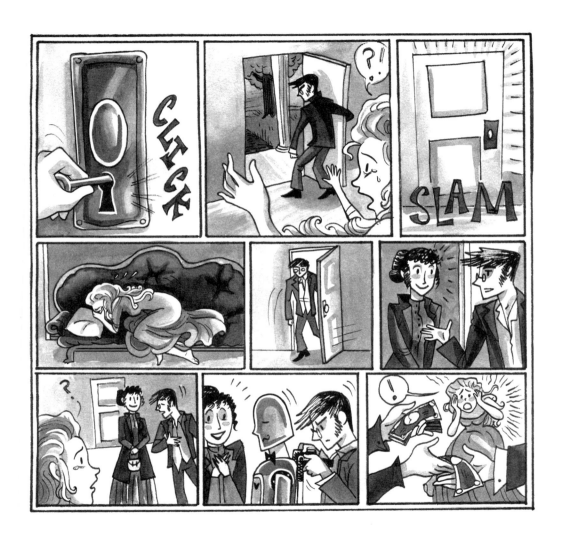

!?
LOCK

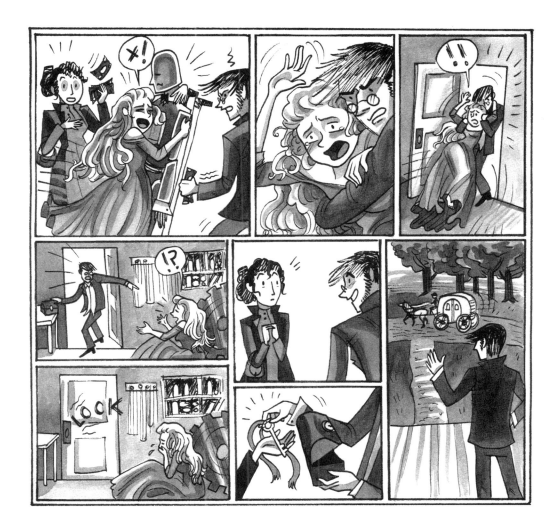

SLAM
?
CHESTER 5000 XYV
Fig.

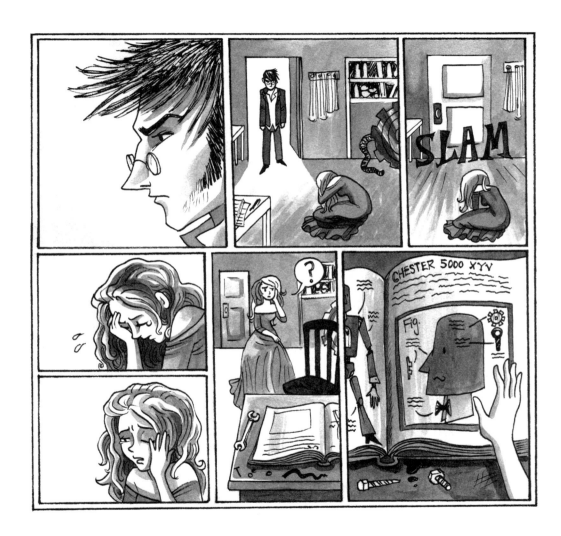

CLICK

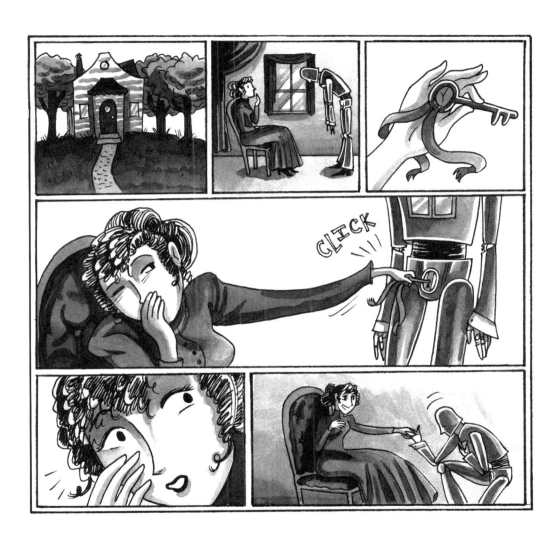

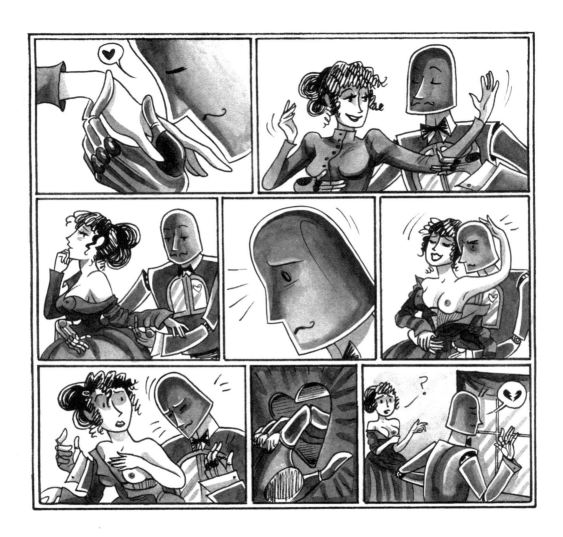

TONK
TONK
TONK
TONK
TONK
TONK TONK
TONK
TONK TONK
TONK
TONK
TONK

TONK TONK TONK
TONK
TONK
!

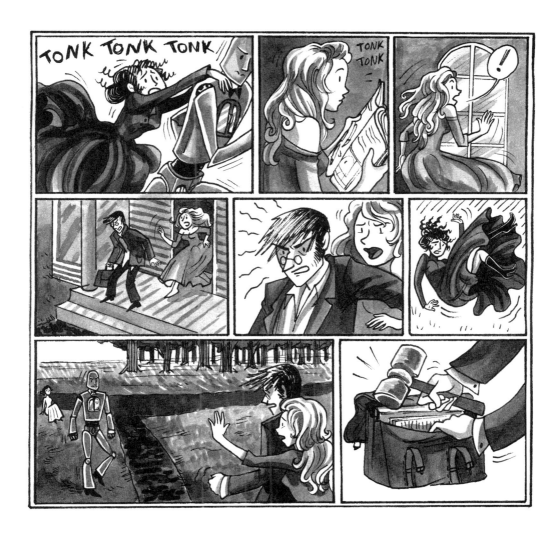

!!!
LANG
PTWAG
TONG
VVVVVVVVV

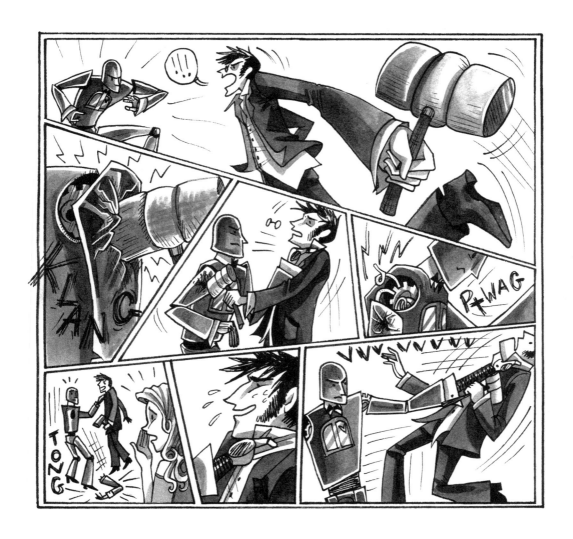

SHWAM
WWWWWWWHHHOOOOOOOOOOOOoo..
!

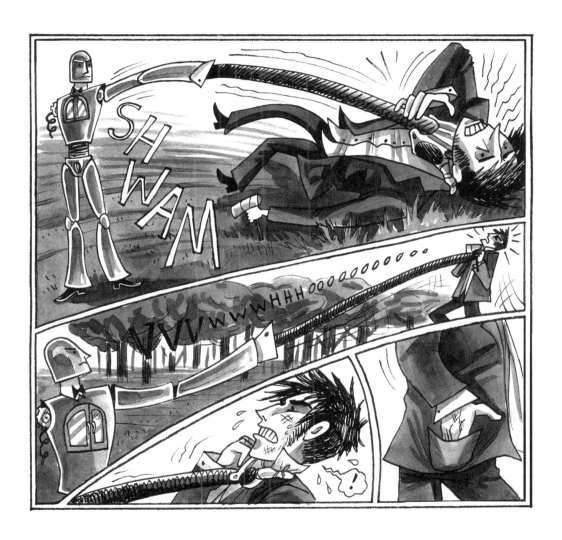

WEDGE
SHWANG

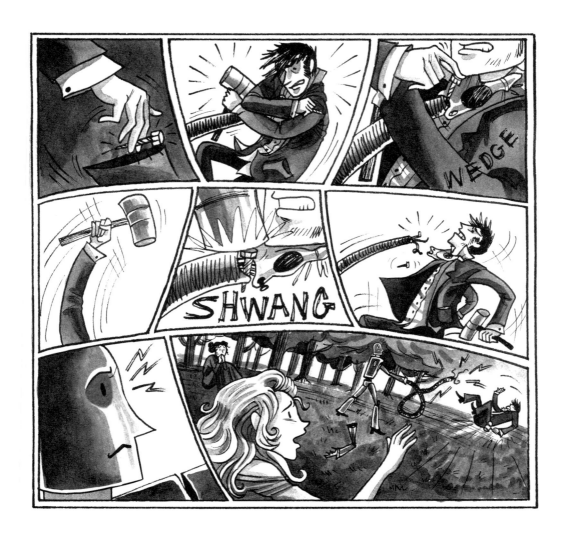

WHAM
SWAKK
CRACK

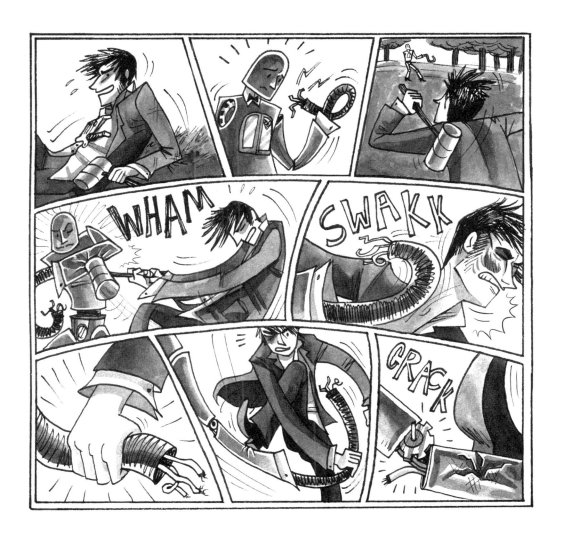

WHOOOOOVVM

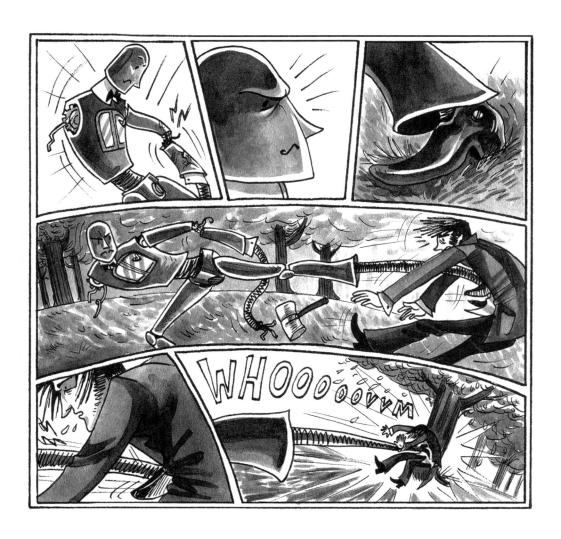

SSSLUUNK
SWAAAAAAA

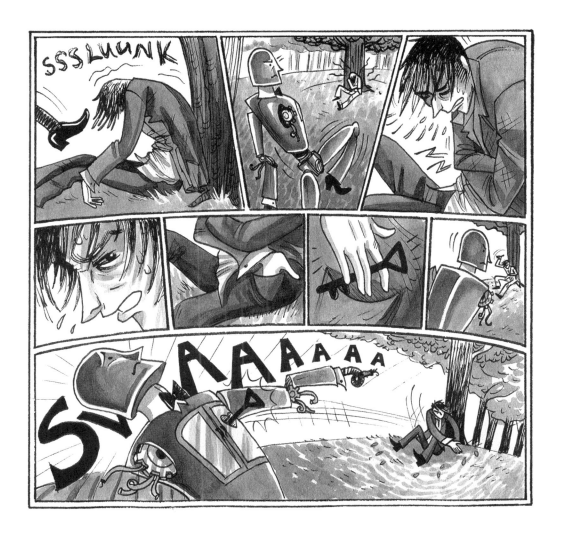

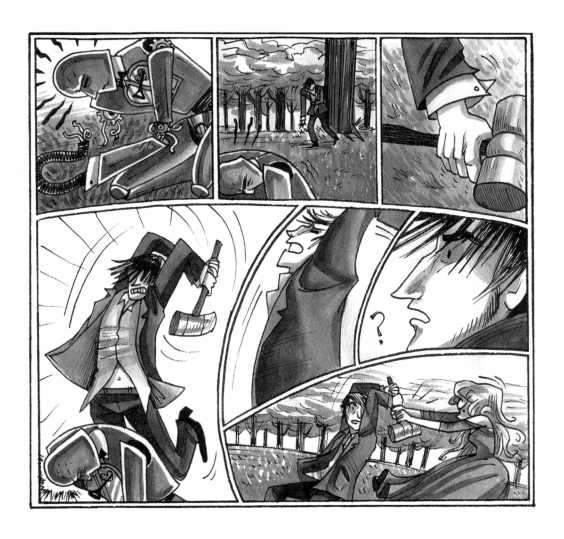

!!!
WHAM

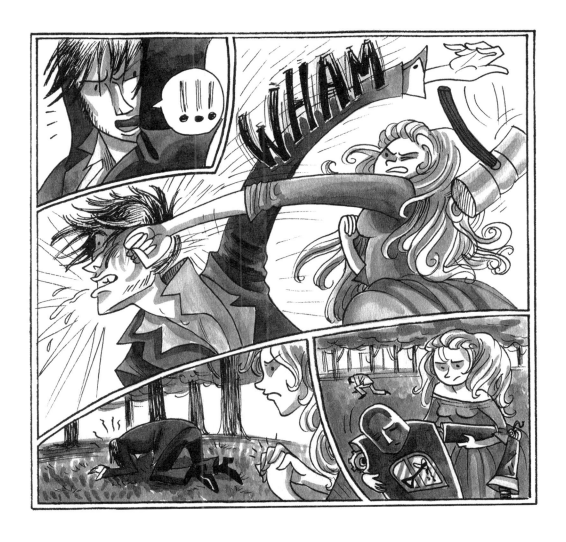

SLAM

CLANG
CLANG
CLANG
FSSSSSSSSSS
SNAP

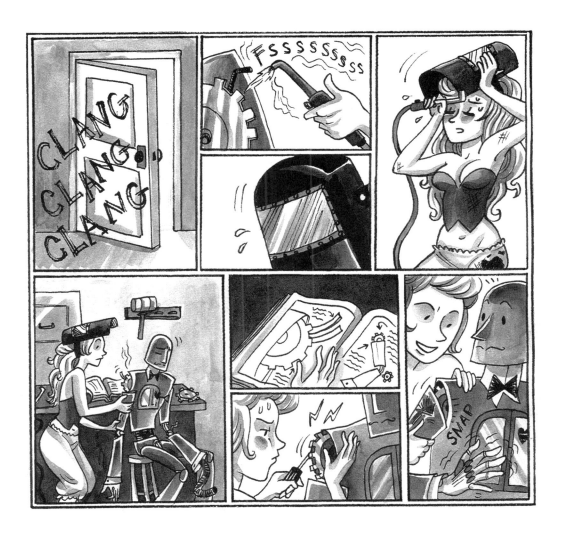

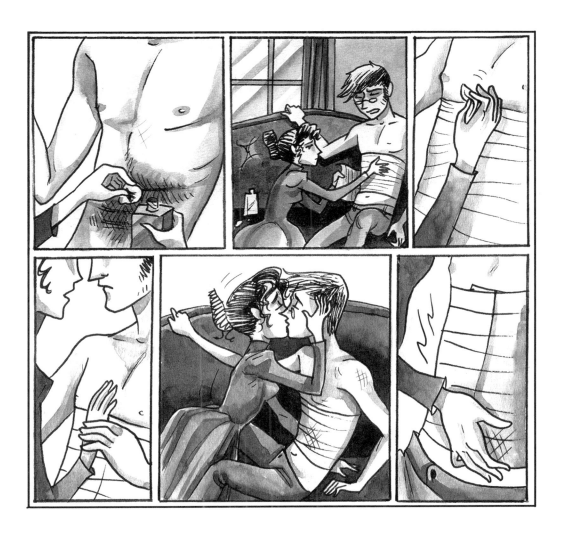

KNOCK
KNOCK
KNOCK
KNOCK

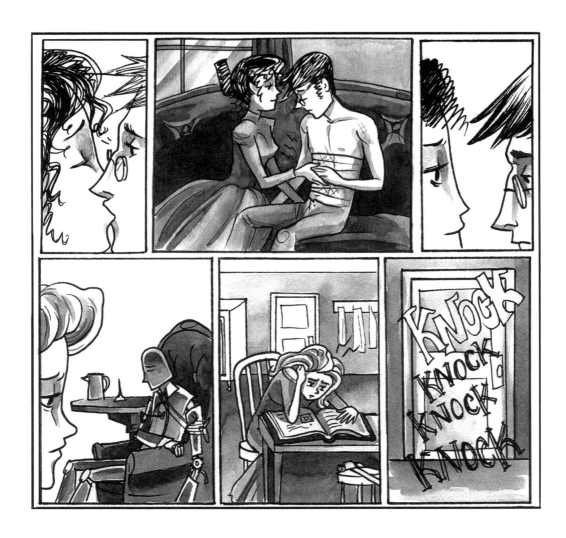

X!

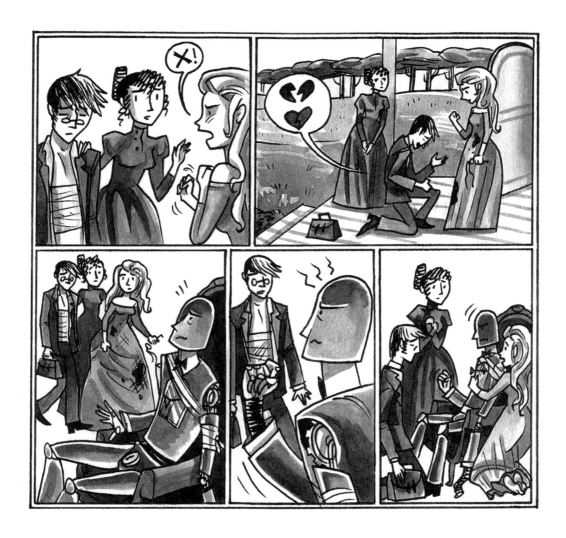

FSSSSHH

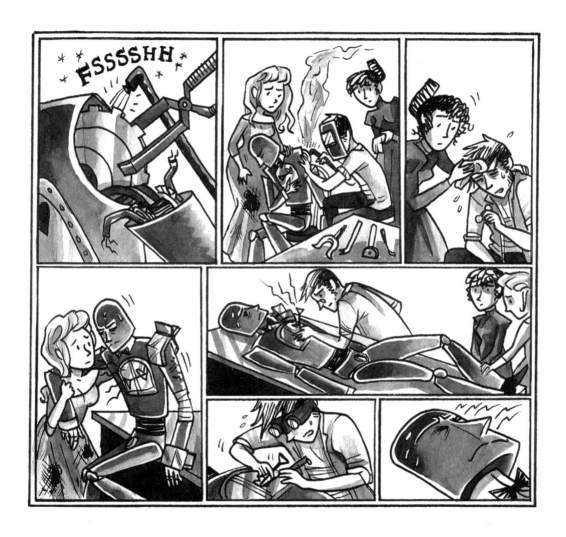

TING

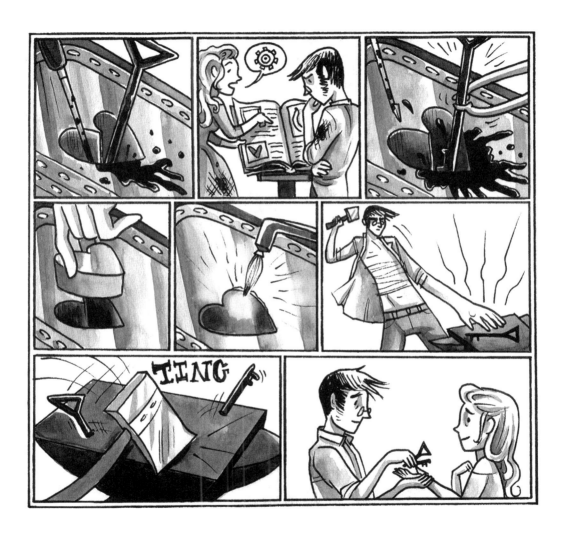

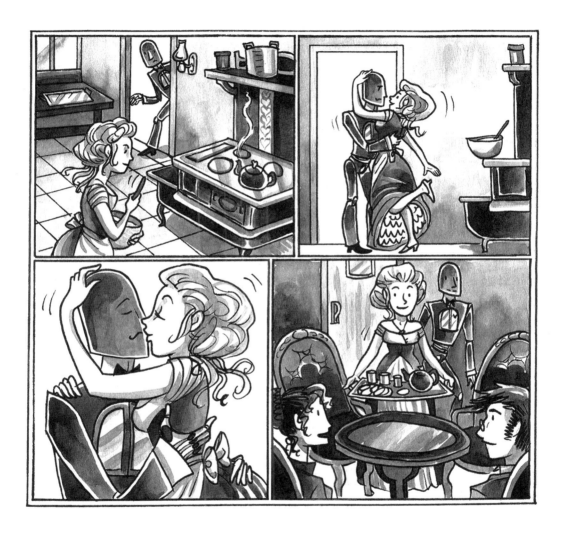

CRUNCH

VWOOOSH!

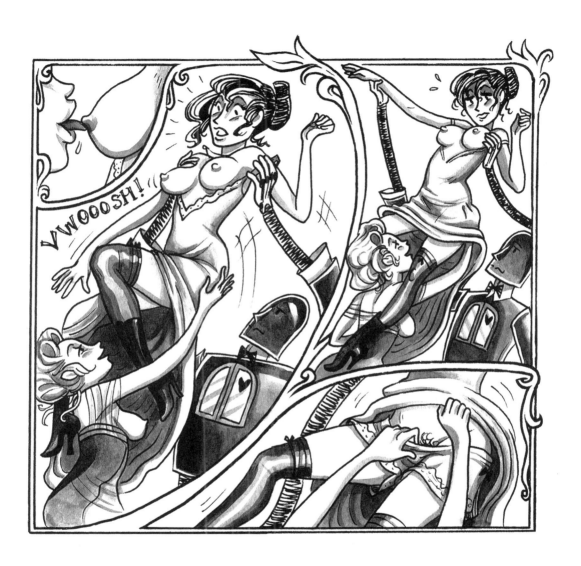

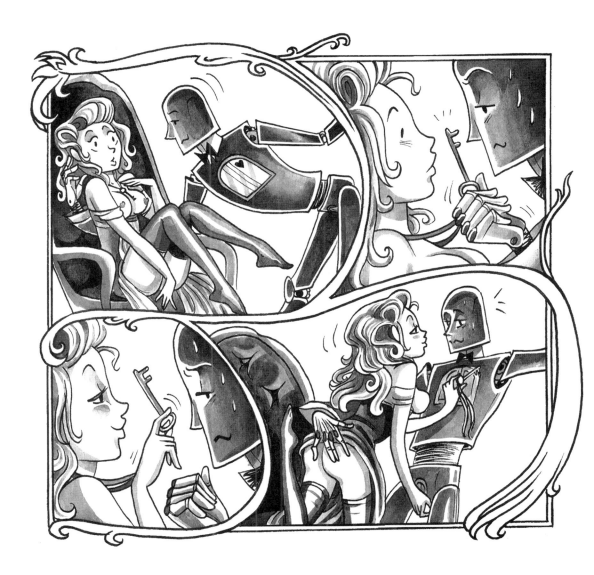

CLICK

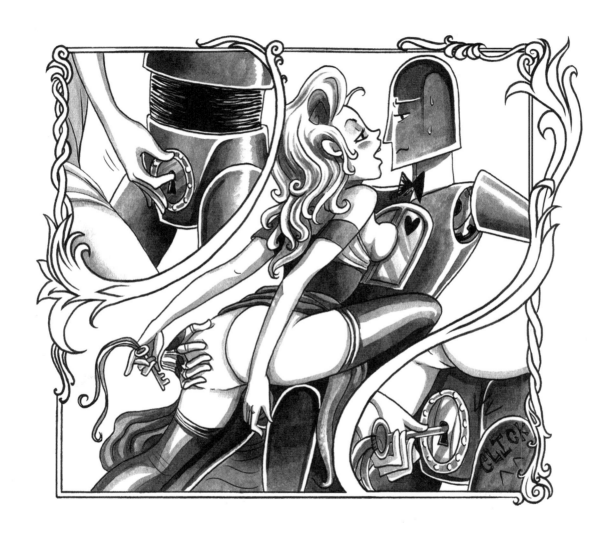

Phallus Auto Extendus
Self Lubricating
Smooth, interlocking circular steel.
Auto Thrusting Pump
fig. 4

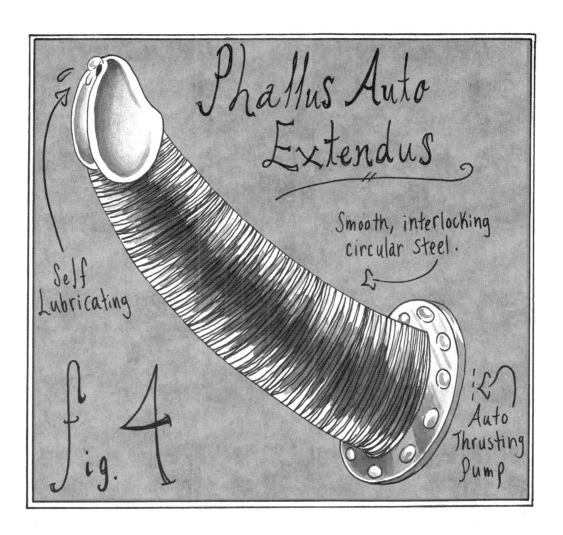

VERTI!

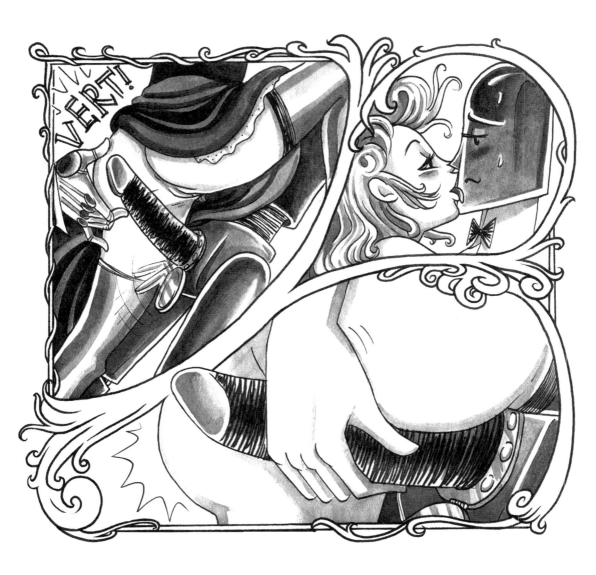

SLIP

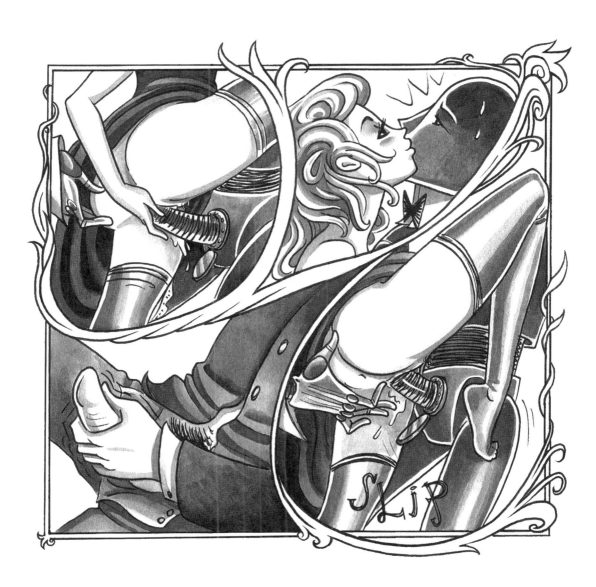

SHWAM!

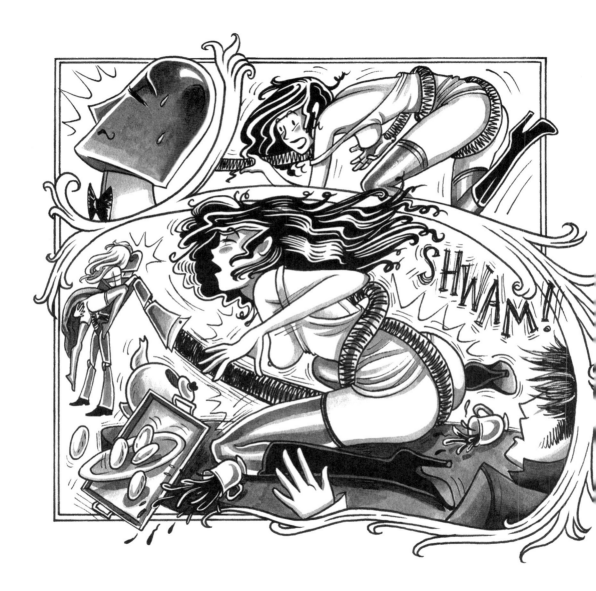

CLICK
WHIIIIRR

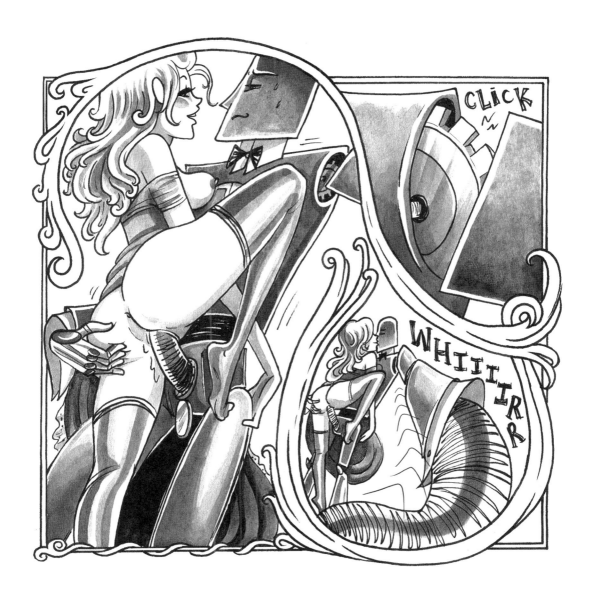

WHIIIIIIIR
?
WHIP
!!

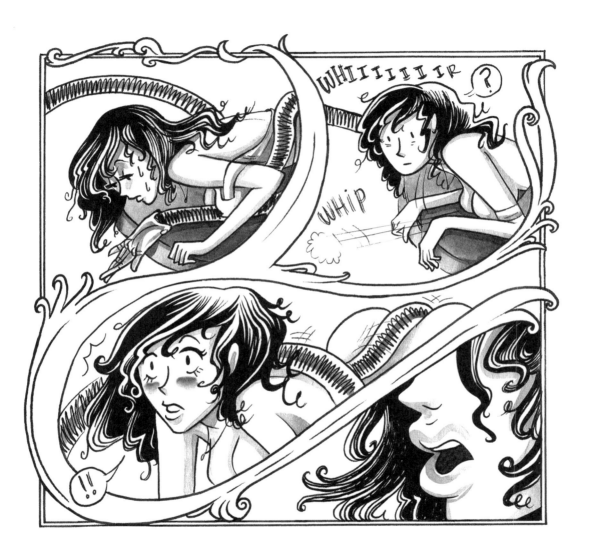

WHIIIIIIRR

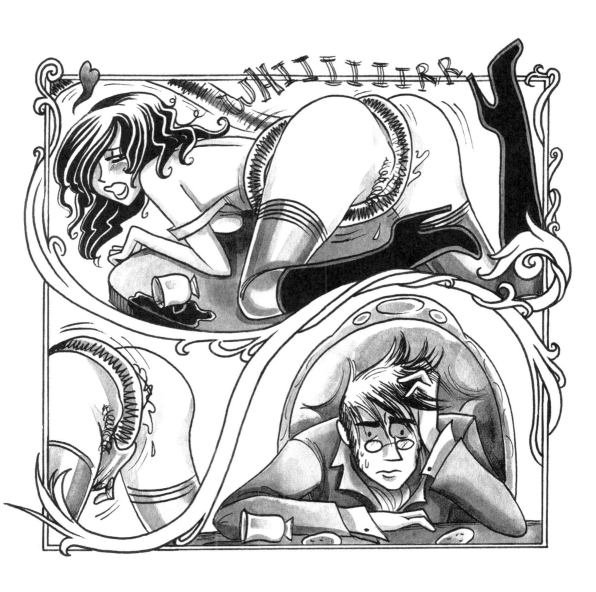

VRRRRRRRRRRR
SNAP
SLAP

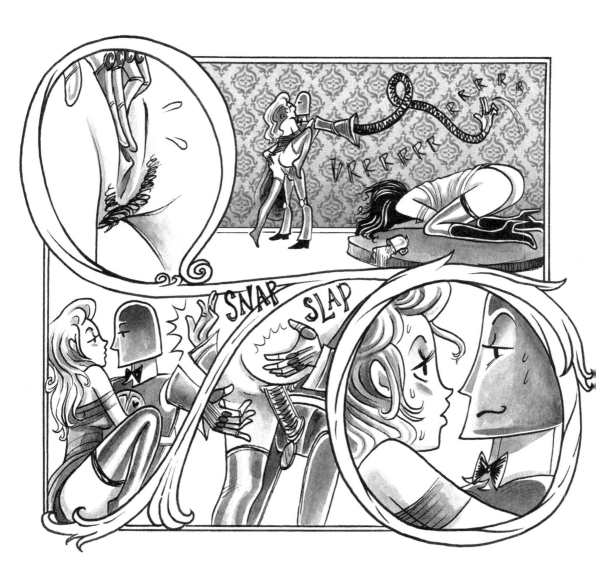

VERT!
♥!!

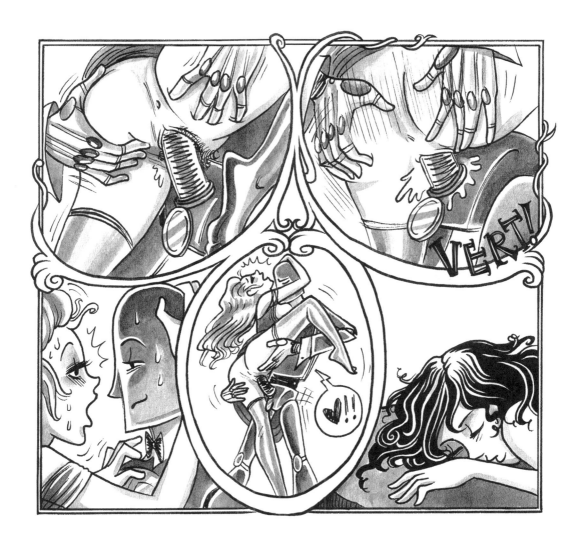

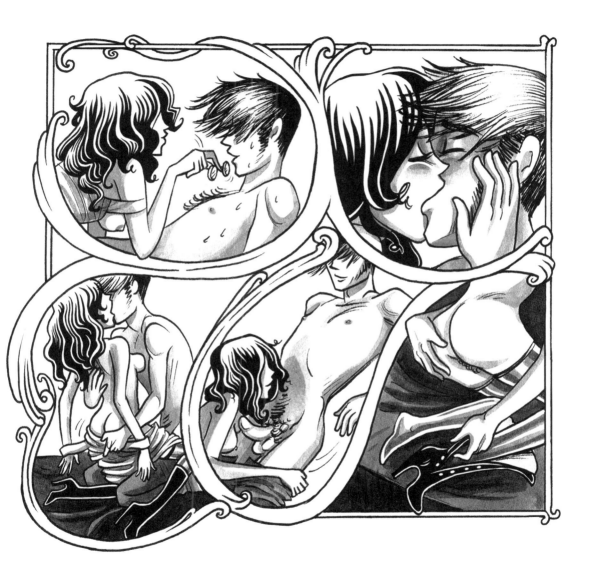

Jess Fink has fornicated with several rainbows, from which she gained her powers. She has been drawing ever since she could hold a pencil, and graduated from the School of Visual Arts in 2003. Her work has appeared in various anthologies, including: *SPX* (2002/2003), *Popgun* volume 4 (Image, 2010), *Best Erotic Comics* (Last Gasp, 2008), and *Erotic Comics* volume 2 (Abrams, 2008). Her erotic work has also been published by Fantagraphics Books.

Her illustration work has been featured in the *New York Times*, and her t-shirts have won the Threadless contest many times. She has always loved drawing sexy unmentionables, but does not shy away from the controversial art of making children's books, of which she has completed two to date.

Jess is a humanist, she can't ride a bike, and she loves marzipan. She lives in New York with her fella and some cats.

Visit Jess's blog: finkenstein.livejournal.com
Read the Chester 5000 webcomic: www.jessfink.com/Chester5000XYV/
or just drop her a line: jessfinkenstein@gmail.com

A Thousand Thank Yous

To Tom Hart, one of the greatest comic storytellers, for encouraging me and telling me I drew "fantastic boobs." To Keith Meyerson for being endlessly positive and teaching me how to be genuine. To my friends and family for putting up with me, and not being too weirded out that I draw porn.

To my amazing webcomics friends, of which there are too many to name, who inspire and delight me every day. To all the erotic artists who have influenced me, who make dirty art and fight against the ridiculous notion that anything sexual isn't art at all. To the unknown artists of the Tijuana Bibles. To various musicians, whose music keeps me drawing late into the night.
To Chris, Brett and Leigh for being great dudes.

And of course, to my amazingly talented fella Eric, my partner in crime.

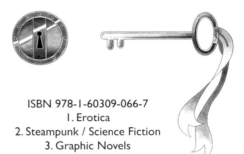

ISBN 978-1-60309-066-7
1. Erotica
2. Steampunk / Science Fiction
3. Graphic Novels

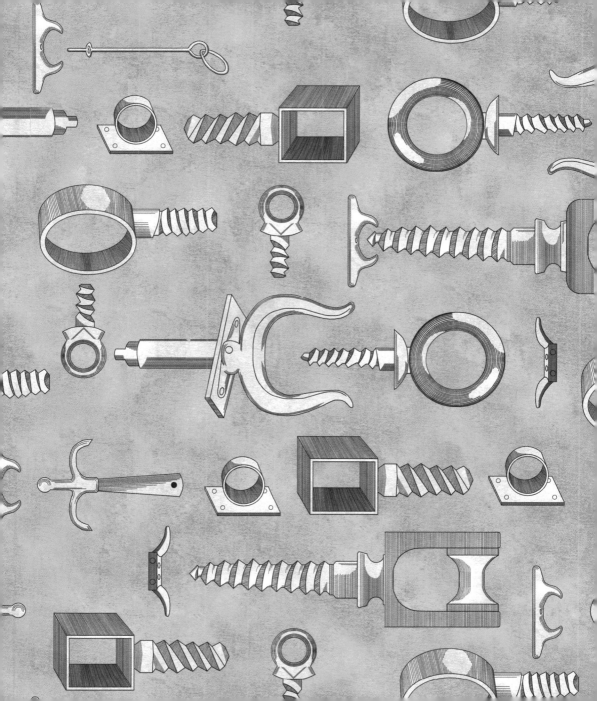

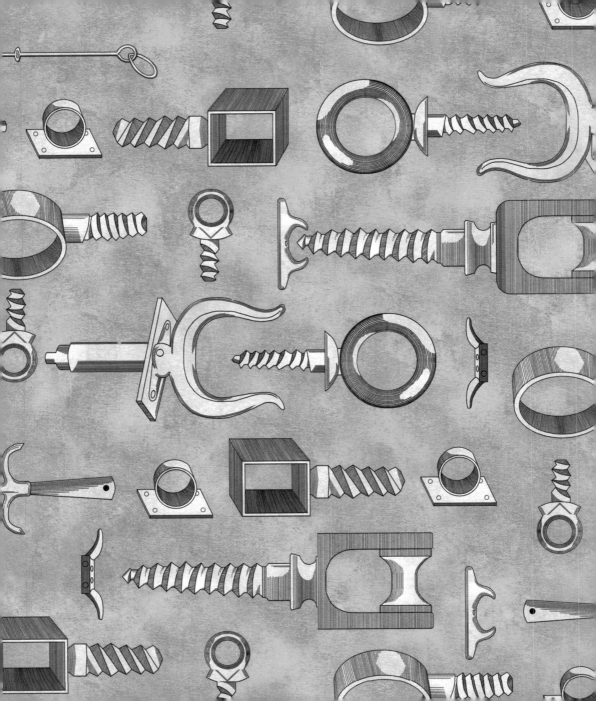